GET READY...GET SET...READ!

HIDE AND SEEK

by
Foster & Erickson

Illustrations by
Kerri Gifford

BARRON'S

"Let's play hide and seek
at the lake," said Blake.

"Fine," said Caroline,
K.C. Swine,
and Porcupine."

"No!" said Sue.
"What would Flute and I do?"

"You cannot hide
if you are big and wide."

"Don't weep, true-blue Sue,"
said Flute.

"I know what we can do."

"Now, who is *IT*?"
asked Blake.

"You are *IT*, Blake!"
said Jake.

Blake closed his eyes
and began to count,
"One, two, three . . ."

Without a peep
they all went to hide.

"Ready or not, here I come!"
cried Blake.

"Now where would they
hide?"

"One, two, three,
on Rose and Lee,
up in the tree."

"Jeepers, Creepers,"
said Lee.

"Here's a good place to hide,
Jake must be asleep inside."

"One, two, three,
on sleepy Jake!"

"Now, who is that I see
behind the pine?"

"It's me,"
said little Porcupine.

"Not *that* pine," said Blake,
"I mean that one!"

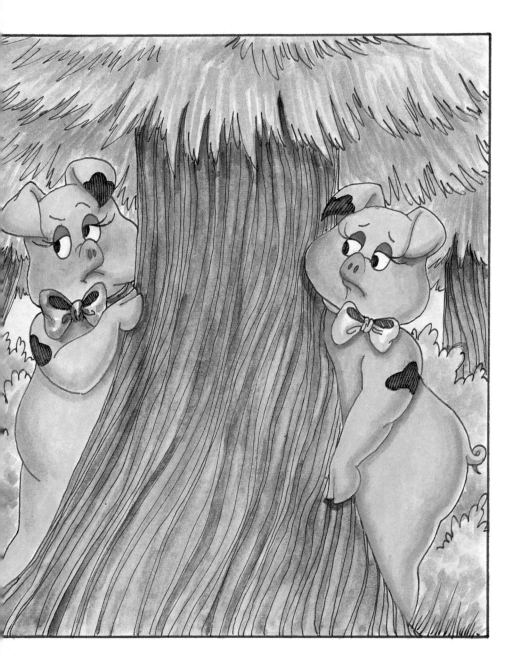

"One, two, three,
on Caroline and K.C.!"

"I don't have a clue where
to find Flute and Sue."

"Wait!" said Blake.
"Did I see the lake shake?"

"The lake is deep and wide,
they *could* hide inside."

"Flute and Sue,
I see you!"

"One, two, three,
on Flute and Sue!"

"One, two, three, on you!"
said Sue.

"I did it! I found you all,"
said Blake.

"Not quite," they said.

"You forgot the snake!"

DEAR PARENTS AND EDUCATORS:

Welcome to *Get Ready...Get Set...Read!*

We've created these books to introduce children to the magic of reading.

Each story in the series is built around one or two word families. For example, *A Mop for Pop* uses the OP word family. Letters and letter blends are added to OP to form words such as TOP, LOP, and STOP.

This *Bring-It-All-Together* book serves as a reading review. When your children have finished *Jake and the Snake*, *Jeepers Creepers*, *Two Fine Swine*, *What Rose Does Not Know*, and *Pink and Blue*, it is time to have them read this book. *Hide and Seek* uses the characters and words introduced in set 3 of *Get Ready . . . Get Set . . . Read!* (Each set in the series will be followed by two review books.)

Bring-It-All-Together books provide:
• much needed vocabulary repetition for developing fluency.
• longer stories for increasing reading attention spans.
• new stories with familiar characters for motivating young readers.

We have created these *Bring-It-All-Together* books to help develop confidence and competence in your young reader. We wish you much success in your reading adventures.

Kelli C. Foster, PhD
Educational Psychologist

Gina Clegg Erickson, MA
Reading Specialist

© Copyright 1995 by Kelli C. Foster, Gina C. Erickson, and Kerri Gifford

All inquiries should be addressed to:
Barron's Educational Series, Inc., 250 Wireless Boulevard, Hauppauge, NY 11788

International Standard Book Number 0-8120-9075-6
Library of Congress Catalog Card Number: 95-15026

Library of Congress Cataloging-in-Publication Data

Foster, Kelli C.
    Hide and seek / by Foster & Erikson ; illustrations by Kerri Gifford.
        p.   cm.—(Get ready— get set— read!)
        Summary: When some animals decide to play hide-and-seek, Blake the raccoon manages to find everyone, except his friend the snake.
        ISBN 0-8120-9075-6
        (1. Hide-and-seek—Fiction. 2. Animals—Fiction. 3. Stories in rhyme.)
    I. Erickson, Gina Clegg. II. Gifford, Kerri, ill. III. Title. IV. Series: Erikson, Gina Clegg. Get ready— get set— read!
    PZ8.3.F813Hi   1995
    (E)—dc20
                                                        95-15026
                                                        CIP
                                                        AC

PRINTED IN HONG KONG
5678   9927   9876543

There are five sets of books in the

Series. Each set consists of five **FIRST BOOKS**
and two **BRING-IT-ALL-TOGETHER BOOKS**.

SET 1

is the first set your children should read.
The word families are selected from the short vowel sounds:
at, **ed**, **ish** and **im**, **op**, **ug**.

SET 2

provides more practice
with short vowel sounds:
an and **and**, **et**, **ip**, **og**, **ub**.

SET 3

focuses on
long vowel sounds:
ake, **eep**, **ide** and **ine**, **oke** and **ose**, **ue** and **ute**.

SET 4

introduces the idea that the word family sounds
can be spelled two different ways:
ale/ail, **een/ean**, **ight/ite**, **ote/oat**, **oon/une**.

SET 5

acquaints children with word families that
do not follow the rules for long and short vowel sounds:
all, **ound**, **y**, **ow**, **ew**.